CON

	Prelude	1
I	Father Zossima's Brother	2
II	Of the Holy Scriptures in the Life of Father Zossima	7
III	Recollections of Father Zossima's Youth before he became a Monk	14
IV	The Mysterious Visitor	23
V	The Russian Monk and his possible Significance	38
VI	Of Masters and Servants, and of whether it is possible for them to be Brothers in the Spirit	41
VII	Of Prayer, Of Love, and of Contact with other Worlds	46
VIII	Can a Man judge his Fellow Creatures? Faith to the End	49
IX	Of Hell and Hell Fire, A Mystic Reflection	51
	Epilogue	53

FYODOR DOSTOYEVSKY

The Life and Teachings of Father Zossima

Translated by CONSTANCE GARNETT

Edited by ALFIE BINGHAM

A Russian Monk

Copyright © Alfie Bingham, 2023

All rights reserved.

ISBN: 9798399193267

HATE NOT EVEN THE WICKED ONES

PRELUDE

Here I must observe that this last conversation of Father Zossima with the friends who visited him on the last day of his life has been partly preserved in writing. Alexey Fyodorovitch Karamazov wrote it down from memory, some time after his elder's death. But whether this was only the conversation that took place then, or whether he added to it his notes of parts of former conversations with his teacher, I cannot determine. In his account, Father Zossima's talk goes on without interruption, as though he told his life to his friends in the form of a story, though there is no doubt, from other accounts of it, that the conversation that evening was general. Though the guests did not interrupt Father Zossima much, yet they too talked, perhaps even told something themselves. Besides, Father Zossima could not have carried on an uninterrupted narrative, for he was sometimes gasping for breath, his voice failed him, and he even lay down to rest on his bed, though he did not fall asleep and his visitors did not leave their seats. Once or twice the conversation was interrupted by Father Païssy's reading the Gospel. It is worthy of note, too, that no one of them supposed that he would die that night, for on that evening of his life after his deep sleep in the day he seemed suddenly to have found new strength, which kept him up through this long conversation. It was like a last effort of love which gave him marvelous energy; only for a little time, however, for his life was cut short immediately.... But of that later. I will only add now that I have preferred to confine myself to the account given by Alexey Fyodorovitch Karamazov. It will be shorter and not so fatiguing, though of course, as I must repeat, Alyosha took a great deal from previous conversations and added them to it.

Notes of the Life of the deceased Priest and Monk, the Elder Zossima, taken from his own words by Alexey Fyodorovitch Karamazov.

I: FATHER ZOSSIMA'S BROTHER

Beloved fathers and teachers, I was born in a distant province in the north, in the town of V. My father was a gentleman by birth, but of no great consequence or position. He died when I was only two years old, and I don't remember him at all. He left my mother a small house built of wood, and a fortune, not large, but sufficient to keep her and her children in comfort. There were two of us, my elder brother Markel and I. He was eight years older than I was, of hasty irritable temperament, but kind-hearted and never ironical. He was remarkably silent, especially at home with me, his mother, and the servants. He did well at school, but did not get on with his schoolfellows, though he never quarreled, at least so my mother has told me. Six months before his death, when he was seventeen, he made friends with a political exile who had been banished from Moscow to our town for freethinking, and led a solitary existence there. He was a good scholar who had gained distinction in philosophy in the university. Something made him take a fancy to Markel, and he used to ask him to see him. The young man would spend whole evenings with him during that winter, till the exile was summoned to Petersburg to take up his post again at his own request, as he had powerful friends.

It was the beginning of Lent, and Markel would not fast, he was rude and laughed at it. "That's all silly twaddle, and there is no God," he said, horrifying my mother, the servants, and me too. For though I was only nine, I too was aghast at hearing such words. We had four servants, all serfs. I remember my mother selling one of the four, the cook Afimya, who was lame and elderly, for sixty paper roubles, and hiring a free servant to take her place.

In the sixth week in Lent, my brother, who was never strong and had a tendency to consumption, was taken ill. He was tall but thin and delicate- looking, and of very pleasing countenance. I suppose he caught cold, anyway the doctor, who came, soon whispered to my mother that it was galloping consumption, that he would not live through the spring. My mother began weeping, and, careful not to alarm my brother, she entreated him to go to church, to confess and take the sacrament, as he was still able to move about. This made him angry, and he said something profane about the church. He grew thoughtful, however; he guessed at once that he was seriously ill, and that that was why his mother was begging him to confess and take the sacrament. He had been aware, indeed, for a long time past, that he was far from well, and had a year before coolly observed at dinner to our mother and me, "My life won't be long among you, I may not live another year," which seemed now like a prophecy.

Three days passed and Holy Week had come. And on Tuesday morning my brother began going to church. "I am doing this simply for your sake, mother, to please and comfort you," he said. My mother wept with joy and grief. "His end must be near," she thought, "if there's such a change in him." But he was not able to go to church long, he took to his bed, so he had to confess and take the sacrament at home.

It was a late Easter, and the days were bright, fine, and full of fragrance. I remember he used to cough all night and sleep badly, but in the morning he dressed and tried to sit up in an arm-chair. That's how I remember him sitting, sweet and gentle, smiling, his face bright and joyous, in spite of his illness. A marvelous change passed over him, his spirit seemed transformed. The old nurse would come in and say, "Let me light the lamp before the holy image, my dear." And once he would not have allowed it and would have blown it out.

"Light it, light it, dear, I was a wretch to have prevented you doing it. You are praying when you light the lamp, and I am praying when I rejoice seeing you. So we are praying to the same God."

Those words seemed strange to us, and mother would go to her room and weep, but when she went in to him she wiped her eyes and looked cheerful. "Mother, don't weep, darling," he would say, "I've long to live yet, long to rejoice with you, and life is glad and joyful."

"Ah, dear boy, how can you talk of joy when you lie feverish at night, coughing as though you would tear yourself to pieces."

"Don't cry, mother," he would answer, "life is paradise, and we are all in paradise, but we won't see it, if we would, we should have heaven on earth the next day."

Every one wondered at his words, he spoke so strangely and positively; we were all touched and wept. Friends came to see us. "Dear ones," he would say to them, "what have I done that you should love me so, how can you love any one like me, and how was it I did not know, I did not appreciate it before?"

When the servants came in to him he would say continually, "Dear, kind people, why are you doing so much for me, do I deserve to be waited on? If it were God's will for me to live, I would wait on you, for all men should wait on one another."

Mother shook her head as she listened. "My darling, it's your illness makes you talk like that."

"Mother, darling," he would say, "there must be servants and masters, but if so I will be the servant of my servants, the same as they are to me. And another thing, mother, every one of us has sinned against all men, and I more than any."

Mother positively smiled at that, smiled through her tears. "Why, how could you have sinned against all men, more than all? Robbers and murderers have done that, but what sin have you committed yet, that you hold yourself more guilty than all?"

"Mother, little heart of mine," he said (he had begun using such strange caressing words at that time), "little heart of mine, my joy, believe me, every one is really responsible to all men for all men and for everything. I don't know how to explain it to you, but I feel it is so, painfully even. And how is it we went on then living, getting angry and not knowing?"

So he would get up every day, more and more sweet and joyous and full of love. When the doctor, an old German called Eisenschmidt, came:

"Well, doctor, have I another day in this world?" he would ask, joking.

"You'll live many days yet," the doctor would answer, "and months and years too."

"Months and years!" he would exclaim. "Why reckon the days? One day is enough for a man to know all happiness. My dear ones, why do we quarrel, try to outshine each other and keep grudges against each other? Let's go straight into the garden, walk and play there, love, appreciate, and kiss each other, and glorify life."

"Your son cannot last long," the doctor told my mother, as she accompanied him to the door. "The disease is affecting his brain."

The windows of his room looked out into the garden, and our garden was a shady one, with old trees in it which were coming into bud. The first birds of spring were flitting in the branches, chirruping and singing at the windows. And looking at them and admiring them, he began suddenly begging their forgiveness too: "Birds of heaven, happy birds, forgive me, for I have sinned against you too." None of us could understand that at the time, but he shed tears of joy. "Yes," he said, "there was such a glory of God all about me: birds, trees, meadows, sky; only I lived in shame and dishonored it all and did not notice the beauty and glory."

"You take too many sins on yourself," mother used to say, weeping.

"Mother, darling, it's for joy, not for grief I am crying. Though I can't explain it to you, I like to humble myself before them, for I don't know how to love them enough. If I have sinned against every one, yet all forgive me, too, and that's heaven. Am I not in heaven now?"

And there was a great deal more I don't remember. I remember I went once into his room when there was no one else there. It was a bright evening, the sun was setting, and the whole room was lighted up. He beckoned me, and I went up to him. He put his hands on my shoulders and looked into my face tenderly, lovingly; he said nothing for a minute, only looked at me like that.

"Well," he said, "run and play now, enjoy life for me too."

I went out then and ran to play. And many times in my life afterwards I remembered even with tears how he told me to enjoy life for him too. There were many other marvelous and beautiful sayings of his, though we did not understand them at the time. He died the third week after Easter. He was fully conscious though he could not talk; up to his last hour he did not change. He looked happy, his eyes beamed and sought us, he smiled at us, beckoned us. There was a great deal of talk even in the town about his death. I was impressed by all this at the time, but not too much so, though I cried a good deal at his funeral. I was young then, a child, but a lasting impression, a hidden feeling of it all, remained in my heart, ready to rise up and respond when the time came. So indeed it happened.

II: OF THE HOLY SCRIPTURES IN THE LIFE OF FATHER ZOSSIMA

I was left alone with my mother. Her friends began advising her to send me to Petersburg as other parents did. "You have only one son now," they said, "and have a fair income, and you will be depriving him perhaps of a brilliant career if you keep him here." They suggested I should be sent to Petersburg to the Cadet Corps, that I might afterwards enter the Imperial Guard. My mother hesitated for a long time, it was awful to part with her only child, but she made up her mind to it at last, though not without many tears, believing she was acting for my happiness. She brought me to Petersburg and put me into the Cadet Corps, and I never saw her again. For she too died three years afterwards. She spent those three years mourning and grieving for both of us.

From the house of my childhood I have brought nothing but precious memories, for there are no memories more precious than those of early childhood in one's first home. And that is almost always so if there is any love and harmony in the family at all. Indeed, precious memories may remain even of a bad home, if only the heart knows how to find what is precious. With my memories of home I count, too, my memories of the Bible, which, child as I was, I was very eager to read at home. I had a book of Scripture history then with excellent pictures, called *A Hundred and Four Stories from the Old and New Testament*, and I learned to read from it. I have it lying on my shelf now, I keep it as a precious relic of the past. But even before I learned to read, I remember first being moved to devotional feeling at eight years old. My mother took me alone to mass (I don't remember where my brother was at the time) on the Monday before Easter. It was a fine day, and I remember to-day, as though I saw it now, how the incense rose from the censer and softly floated upwards and, overhead in the cupola, mingled in rising waves with the sunlight that streamed in at the little window. I was stirred by the sight, and for the first time in my life I consciously received the seed of God's word in my heart. A youth came out into the middle of the church carrying a big book, so large that at the time I fancied he could scarcely carry it. He laid it on the reading desk, opened it, and began reading, and suddenly for the first time I understood something read in the church of God. In the land of Uz, there lived a man, righteous and God-fearing, and he had great wealth, so many camels, so many sheep and asses, and his children feasted, and he loved them very much and prayed for them. "It may be that my sons have sinned in their feasting." Now the devil came before the Lord together with the sons of God, and said to the Lord that he had gone up and down the earth and under the earth. "And hast thou considered my servant Job?" God asked of him. And God boasted to the devil, pointing to his great and holy servant. And the devil laughed at God's words. "Give him over to me and Thou wilt see that Thy servant will murmur against Thee and curse Thy name." And God gave up the just man He loved so, to the devil. And the devil smote his children and his cattle and scattered his wealth, all of a sudden like a thunderbolt from heaven. And Job rent his mantle and fell down upon the ground and cried aloud, "Naked came I out of my mother's womb, and naked shall I return into the earth; the Lord gave and the Lord has taken away. Blessed be the name of the Lord for ever and ever."

Fathers and teachers, forgive my tears now, for all my childhood rises up again before me, and I breathe now as I breathed then, with the breast of a little child of eight, and I feel as I did then, awe and wonder and gladness. The camels at that time caught my imagination, and Satan, who talked like that with God, and God who gave His servant up to destruction, and His servant crying out: "Blessed be Thy name although Thou dost punish me," and then the soft and sweet singing in the church: "Let my prayer rise up before Thee," and again incense from the priest's censer and the kneeling and the prayer. Ever since then— only yesterday I took it up—I've never been able to read that sacred tale without tears. And how much that is great, mysterious and unfathomable there is in it! Afterwards I heard the words of mockery and blame, proud words, "How could God give up the most loved of His saints for the diversion of the devil, take from him his children, smite him with sore boils so that he cleansed the corruption from his sores with a pot-sherd—and for no object except to boast to the devil! 'See what My saint can suffer for My sake.' " But the greatness of it lies just in the fact that it is a mystery—that the passing earthly show and the eternal verity are brought together in it. In the face of the earthly truth, the eternal truth is accomplished. The Creator, just as on the first days of creation He ended each day with praise: "That is good that I have created," looks upon Job and again praises His creation. And Job, praising the Lord, serves not only Him but all His creation for generations and generations, and for ever and ever, since for that he was ordained. Good heavens, what a book it is, and what lessons there are in it! What a book the Bible is, what a miracle, what strength is given with it to man! It is like a mold cast of the world and man and human nature, everything is there, and a law for everything for all the ages. And what mysteries are solved and revealed! God raises Job again, gives him wealth again. Many years pass by, and he has other children and loves them. But how could he love those new ones when those first children are no more, when he has lost them? Remembering them, how could he be fully happy with those new ones, however dear the new ones might be? But he could, he could. It's the great mystery of human life that old grief passes gradually into quiet, tender joy. The mild serenity of age takes the place of the riotous blood of youth. I bless the rising sun each day, and, as before, my hearts sings to meet it, but now I love even more its setting, its long slanting rays and the soft, tender, gentle memories that come with them, the dear images from the whole of my long, happy life—and over all the Divine Truth, softening, reconciling, forgiving! My life is ending, I know that well, but every day that is left me I feel how my earthly life is in touch with a new infinite, unknown, that approaching life, the nearness of which sets my soul quivering with rapture, my mind glowing and my heart weeping with joy.

Friends and teachers, I have heard more than once, and of late one may hear it more often, that the priests, and above all the village priests, are complaining on all sides of their miserable income and their humiliating lot. They plainly state, even in print—I've read it myself—that they are unable to teach the Scriptures to the people because of the smallness of their means, and if Lutherans and heretics come and lead the flock astray, they let them lead them astray because they have so little to live upon. May the Lord increase the sustenance that is so precious to them, for their complaint is just, too. But of a truth I say, if any one is to blame in the matter, half the fault is ours. For he may be short of time, he may say truly that he is overwhelmed all the while with work and services, but still it's not all the time, even he has an hour a week to remember God. And he does not work the whole year round. Let him gather round him once a week, some hour in the evening, if only the children at first—the fathers will hear of it and they too will begin to come. There's no need to build halls for this, let him take them into his own cottage. They won't spoil his cottage, they would only be there one hour. Let him open that book and begin reading it without grand words or superciliousness, without condescension to them, but gently and kindly, being glad that he is reading to them and that they are listening with attention, loving the words himself, only stopping from time to time to explain words that are not understood by the peasants. Don't be anxious, they will understand everything, the orthodox heart will understand all! Let him read them about Abraham and Sarah, about Isaac and Rebecca, of how Jacob went to Laban and wrestled with the Lord in his dream and said, "This place is holy"—and he will impress the devout mind of the peasant. Let him read, especially to the children, how the brothers sold Joseph, the tender boy, the dreamer and prophet, into bondage, and told their father that a wild beast had devoured him, and showed him his blood- stained clothes. Let him read them how the brothers afterwards journeyed into Egypt for corn, and Joseph, already a great ruler, unrecognized by them, tormented them, accused them, kept his brother Benjamin, and all through love: "I love you, and loving you I torment you." For he remembered all his life how they had sold him to the merchants in the burning desert by the well, and how, wringing his hands, he had wept and besought his brothers not to sell him as a slave in a strange land. And how, seeing them again after many years, he loved them beyond measure, but he harassed and tormented them in love. He left them at last not able to bear the suffering of his heart, flung himself on his bed and wept. Then, wiping his tears away, he went out to them joyful and told them, "Brothers, I am your brother Joseph!" Let him read them further how happy old Jacob was on learning that his darling boy was still alive, and how he went to Egypt leaving his own country, and died in a foreign land, bequeathing his great prophecy that had lain mysteriously hidden in his meek and timid heart all his life, that from his offspring, from Judah, will come the great hope of the world, the Messiah and Saviour.

Fathers and teachers, forgive me and don't be angry, that like a little child I've been babbling of what you know long ago, and can teach me a hundred times more skillfully. I only speak from rapture, and forgive my tears, for I love the Bible. Let him too weep, the priest of God, and be sure that the hearts of his listeners will throb in response. Only a little tiny seed is needed—drop it into the heart of the peasant and it won't die, it will live in his soul all his life, it will be hidden in the midst of his darkness and sin, like a bright spot, like a great reminder. And there's no need of much teaching or explanation, he will understand it all simply. Do you suppose that the peasants don't understand? Try reading them the touching story of the fair Esther and the haughty Vashti; or the miraculous story of Jonah in the whale. Don't forget either the parables of Our Lord, choose especially from the Gospel of St. Luke (that is what I did), and then from the Acts of the Apostles the conversion of St. Paul (that you mustn't leave out on any account), and from the *Lives of the Saints*, for instance, the life of Alexey, the man of God and, greatest of all, the happy martyr and the seer of God, Mary of Egypt—and you will penetrate their hearts with these simple tales. Give one hour a week to it in spite of your poverty, only one little hour. And you will see for yourselves that our people is gracious and grateful, and will repay you a hundred-fold. Mindful of the kindness of their priest and the moving words they have heard from him, they will of their own accord help him in his fields and in his house, and will treat him with more respect than before—so that it will even increase his worldly well-being too. The thing is so simple that sometimes one is even afraid to put it into words, for fear of being laughed at, and yet how true it is! One who does not believe in God will not believe in God's people. He who believes in God's people will see His Holiness too, even though he had not believed in it till then. Only the people and their future spiritual power will convert our atheists, who have torn themselves away from their native soil.

And what is the use of Christ's words, unless we set an example? The people is lost without the Word of God, for its soul is athirst for the Word and for all that is good.

In my youth, long ago, nearly forty years ago, I traveled all over Russia with Father Anfim, collecting funds for our monastery, and we stayed one night on the bank of a great navigable river with some fishermen. A good- looking peasant lad, about eighteen, joined us; he had to hurry back next morning to pull a merchant's barge along the bank. I noticed him looking straight before him with clear and tender eyes. It was a bright, warm, still, July night, a cool mist rose from the broad river, we could hear the plash of a fish, the birds were still, all was hushed and beautiful, everything praying to God. Only we two were not sleeping, the lad and I, and we talked of the beauty of this world of God's and of the great mystery of it. Every blade of grass, every insect, ant, and golden bee, all so marvelously know their path, though they have not intelligence, they bear witness to the mystery of God and continually accomplish it themselves. I saw the dear lad's heart was moved. He told me that he loved the forest and the forest birds. He was a bird-catcher, knew the note of each of them, could call each bird. "I know nothing better than to be in the forest," said he, "though all things are good."

"Truly," I answered him, "all things are good and fair, because all is truth. Look," said I, "at the horse, that great beast that is so near to man; or the lowly, pensive ox, which feeds him and works for him; look at their faces, what meekness, what devotion to man, who often beats them mercilessly. What gentleness, what confidence and what beauty! It's touching to know that there's no sin in them, for all, all except man, is sinless, and Christ has been with them before us."

"Why," asked the boy, "is Christ with them too?"

"It cannot but be so," said I, "since the Word is for all. All creation and all creatures, every leaf is striving to the Word, singing glory to God, weeping to Christ, unconsciously accomplishing this by the mystery of their sinless life. Yonder," said I, "in the forest wanders the dreadful bear, fierce and menacing, and yet innocent in it." And I told him how once a bear came to a great saint who had taken refuge in a tiny cell in the wood. And the great saint pitied him, went up to him without fear and gave him a piece of bread. "Go along," said he, "Christ be with you," and the savage beast walked away meekly and obediently, doing no harm. And the lad was delighted that the bear had walked away without hurting the saint, and that Christ was with him too. "Ah," said he, "how good that is, how good and beautiful is all God's work!" He sat musing softly and sweetly. I saw he understood. And he slept beside me a light and sinless sleep. May God bless youth! And I prayed for him as I went to sleep. Lord, send peace and light to Thy people!

III: RECOLLECTIONS OF FATHER ZOSSIMA'S YOUTH BEFORE HE BECAME A MONK

I spent a long time, almost eight years, in the military cadet school at Petersburg, and in the novelty of my surroundings there, many of my childish impressions grew dimmer, though I forgot nothing. I picked up so many new habits and opinions that I was transformed into a cruel, absurd, almost savage creature. A surface polish of courtesy and society manners I did acquire together with the French language.

But we all, myself included, looked upon the soldiers in our service as cattle. I was perhaps worse than the rest in that respect, for I was so much more impressionable than my companions. By the time we left the school as officers, we were ready to lay down our lives for the honor of the regiment, but no one of us had any knowledge of the real meaning of honor, and if any one had known it, he would have been the first to ridicule it. Drunkenness, debauchery and devilry were what we almost prided ourselves on. I don't say that we were bad by nature, all these young men were good fellows, but they behaved badly, and I worst of all. What made it worse for me was that I had come into my own money, and so I flung myself into a life of pleasure, and plunged headlong into all the recklessness of youth.

I was fond of reading, yet strange to say, the Bible was the one book I never opened at that time, though I always carried it about with me, and I was never separated from it; in very truth I was keeping that book "for the day and the hour, for the month and the year," though I knew it not.

After four years of this life, I chanced to be in the town of K. where our regiment was stationed at the time. We found the people of the town hospitable, rich and fond of entertainments. I met with a cordial reception everywhere, as I was of a lively temperament and was known to be well off, which always goes a long way in the world. And then a circumstance happened which was the beginning of it all.

I formed an attachment to a beautiful and intelligent young girl of noble and lofty character, the daughter of people much respected. They were well-to-do people of influence and position. They always gave me a cordial and friendly reception. I fancied that the young lady looked on me with favor and my heart was aflame at such an idea. Later on I saw and fully realized that I perhaps was not so passionately in love with her at all, but only recognized the elevation of her mind and character, which I could not indeed have helped doing. I was prevented, however, from making her an offer at the time by my selfishness, I was loath to part with the allurements of my free and licentious bachelor life in the heyday of my youth, and with my pockets full of money. I did drop some hint as to my feelings however, though I put off taking any decisive step for a time. Then, all of a sudden, we were ordered off for two months to another district.

On my return two months later, I found the young lady already married to a rich neighboring landowner, a very amiable man, still young though older than I was, connected with the best Petersburg society, which I was not, and of excellent education, which I also was not. I was so overwhelmed at this unexpected circumstance that my mind was positively clouded. The worst of it all was that, as I learned then, the young landowner had been a long while betrothed to her, and I had met him indeed many times in her house, but blinded by my conceit I had noticed nothing. And this particularly mortified me; almost everybody had known all about it, while I knew nothing. I was filled with sudden irrepressible fury. With flushed face I began recalling how often I had been on the point of declaring my love to her, and as she had not attempted to stop me or to warn me, she must, I concluded, have been laughing at me all the time. Later on, of course, I reflected and remembered that she had been very far from laughing at me; on the contrary, she used to turn off any love-making on my part with a jest and begin talking of other subjects; but at that moment I was incapable of reflecting and was all eagerness for revenge. I am surprised to remember that my wrath and revengeful feelings were extremely repugnant to my own nature, for being of an easy temper, I found it difficult to be angry with any one for long, and so I had to work myself up artificially and became at last revolting and absurd.

I waited for an opportunity and succeeded in insulting my "rival" in the presence of a large company. I insulted him on a perfectly extraneous pretext, jeering at his opinion upon an important public event—it was in the year 1826[5]—and my jeer was, so people said, clever and effective. Then I forced him to ask for an explanation, and behaved so rudely that he accepted my challenge in spite of the vast inequality between us, as I was younger, a person of no consequence, and of inferior rank. I learned afterwards for a fact that it was from a jealous feeling on his side also that my challenge was accepted; he had been rather jealous of me on his wife's account before their marriage; he fancied now that if he submitted to be insulted by me and refused to accept my challenge, and if she heard of it, she might begin to despise him and waver in her love for him. I soon found a second in a comrade, an ensign of our regiment. In those days though duels were severely punished, yet dueling was a kind of fashion among the officers—so strong and deeply rooted will a brutal prejudice sometimes be.

It was the end of June, and our meeting was to take place at seven o'clock the next day on the outskirts of the town—and then something happened that in very truth was the turning-point of my life. In the evening, returning home in a savage and brutal humor, I flew into a rage with my orderly Afanasy, and gave him two blows in the face with all my might, so that it was covered with blood. He had not long been in my service and I had struck him before, but never with such ferocious cruelty. And, believe me, though it's forty years ago, I recall it now with shame and pain. I went to bed and slept for about three hours; when I waked up the day was breaking. I got up—I did not want to sleep any more—I went to the window—opened it, it looked out upon the garden; I saw the sun rising; it was warm and beautiful, the birds were singing.

"What's the meaning of it?" I thought. "I feel in my heart as it were something vile and shameful. Is it because I am going to shed blood? No," I thought, "I feel it's not that. Can it be that I am afraid of death, afraid of being killed? No, that's not it, that's not it at all."... And all at once I knew what it was: it was because I had beaten Afanasy the evening before! It all rose before my mind, it all was as it were repeated over again; he stood before me and I was beating him straight on the face and he was holding his arms stiffly down, his head erect, his eyes fixed upon me as though on parade. He staggered at every blow and did not even dare to raise his hands to protect himself. That is what a man has been brought to, and that was a man beating a fellow creature! What a crime! It was as though a sharp dagger had pierced me right through. I stood as if I were struck dumb, while the sun was shining, the leaves were rejoicing and the birds were trilling the praise of God.... I hid my face in my hands, fell on my bed and broke into a storm of tears. And then I remembered my brother Markel and what he said on his death-bed to his servants: "My dear ones, why do you wait on me, why do you love me, am I worth your waiting on me?"

"Yes, am I worth it?" flashed through my mind. "After all what am I worth, that another man, a fellow creature, made in the likeness and image of God, should serve me?" For the first time in my life this question forced itself upon me. He had said, "Mother, my little heart, in truth we are each responsible to all for all, it's only that men don't know this. If they knew it, the world would be a paradise at once."

"God, can that too be false?" I thought as I wept. "In truth, perhaps, I am more than all others responsible for all, a greater sinner than all men in the world." And all at once the whole truth in its full light appeared to me; what was I going to do? I was going to kill a good, clever, noble man, who had done me no wrong, and by depriving his wife of happiness for the rest of her life, I should be torturing and killing her too. I lay thus in my bed with my face in the pillow, heedless how the time was passing. Suddenly my second, the ensign, came in with the pistols to fetch me.

"Ah," said he, "it's a good thing you are up already, it's time we were off, come along!"

I did not know what to do and hurried to and fro undecided; we went out to the carriage, however.

"Wait here a minute," I said to him. "I'll be back directly, I have forgotten my purse."

And I ran back alone, to Afanasy's little room.

"Afanasy," I said, "I gave you two blows on the face yesterday, forgive me," I said.

He started as though he were frightened, and looked at me; and I saw that it was not enough, and on the spot, in my full officer's uniform, I dropped at his feet and bowed my head to the ground.

"Forgive me," I said.

Then he was completely aghast.

"Your honor ... sir, what are you doing? Am I worth it?"

And he burst out crying as I had done before, hid this face in his hands, turned to the window and shook all over with his sobs. I flew out to my comrade and jumped into the carriage.

"Ready," I cried. "Have you ever seen a conqueror?" I asked him. "Here is one before you."

I was in ecstasy, laughing and talking all the way, I don't remember what about.

He looked at me. "Well, brother, you are a plucky fellow, you'll keep up the honor of the uniform, I can see."

So we reached the place and found them there, waiting us. We were placed twelve paces apart; he had the first shot. I stood gayly, looking him full in the face; I did not twitch an eyelash, I looked lovingly at him, for I knew what I would do. His shot just grazed my cheek and ear.

"Thank God," I cried, "no man has been killed," and I seized my pistol, turned back and flung it far away into the wood. "That's the place for you," I cried.

I turned to my adversary.

"Forgive me, young fool that I am, sir," I said, "for my unprovoked insult to you and for forcing you to fire at me. I am ten times worse than you and more, maybe. Tell that to the person whom you hold dearest in the world."

I had no sooner said this than they all three shouted at me.

"Upon my word," cried my adversary, annoyed, "if you did not want to fight, why did not you let me alone?"

"Yesterday I was a fool, to-day I know better," I answered him gayly.

"As to yesterday, I believe you, but as for to-day, it is difficult to agree with your opinion," said he.

"Bravo," I cried, clapping my hands. "I agree with you there too. I have deserved it!"

"Will you shoot, sir, or not?"

"No, I won't," I said; "if you like, fire at me again, but it would be better for you not to fire."

The seconds, especially mine, were shouting too: "Can you disgrace the regiment like this, facing your antagonist and begging his forgiveness! If I'd only known this!"

I stood facing them all, not laughing now.

"Gentlemen," I said, "is it really so wonderful in these days to find a man who can repent of his stupidity and publicly confess his wrongdoing?"

"But not in a duel," cried my second again.

"That's what's so strange," I said. "For I ought to have owned my fault as soon as I got here, before he had fired a shot, before leading him into a great and deadly sin; but we have made our life so grotesque, that to act in that way would have been almost impossible, for only after I have faced his shot at the distance of twelve paces could my words have any significance for him, and if I had spoken before, he would have said, 'He is a coward, the sight of the pistols has frightened him, no use to listen to him.' Gentlemen," I cried suddenly, speaking straight from my heart, "look around you at the gifts of God, the clear sky, the pure air, the tender grass, the birds; nature is beautiful and sinless, and we, only we, are sinful and foolish, and we don't understand that life is heaven, for we have only to understand that and it will at once be fulfilled in all its beauty, we shall embrace each other and weep."

I would have said more but I could not; my voice broke with the sweetness and youthful gladness of it, and there was such bliss in my heart as I had never known before in my life.

"All this as rational and edifying," said my antagonist, "and in any case you are an original person."

"You may laugh," I said to him, laughing too, "but afterwards you will approve of me."

"Oh, I am ready to approve of you now," said he; "will you shake hands? for I believe you are genuinely sincere."

"No," I said, "not now, later on when I have grown worthier and deserve your esteem, then shake hands and you will do well."

We went home, my second upbraiding me all the way, while I kissed him. All my comrades heard of the affair at once and gathered together to pass judgment on me the same day.

"He has disgraced the uniform," they said; "let him resign his commission."

Some stood up for me: "He faced the shot," they said.

"Yes, but he was afraid of his other shot and begged for forgiveness."

"If he had been afraid of being shot, he would have shot his own pistol first before asking forgiveness, while he flung it loaded into the forest. No, there's something else in this, something original."

I enjoyed listening and looking at them. "My dear friends and comrades," said I, "don't worry about my resigning my commission, for I have done so already. I have sent in my papers this morning and as soon as I get my discharge I shall go into a monastery—it's with that object I am leaving the regiment."

When I had said this every one of them burst out laughing.

"You should have told us of that first, that explains everything, we can't judge a monk."

They laughed and could not stop themselves, and not scornfully, but kindly and merrily. They all felt friendly to me at once, even those who had been sternest in their censure, and all the following month, before my discharge came, they could not make enough of me. "Ah, you monk," they would say. And every one said something kind to me, they began trying to dissuade me, even to pity me: "What are you doing to yourself?"

"No," they would say, "he is a brave fellow, he faced fire and could have fired his own pistol too, but he had a dream the night before that he should become a monk, that's why he did it."

It was the same thing with the society of the town. Till then I had been kindly received, but had not been the object of special attention, and now all came to know me at once and invited me; they laughed at me, but they loved me. I may mention that although everybody talked openly of our duel, the authorities took no notice of it, because my antagonist was a near relation of our general, and as there had been no bloodshed and no serious consequences, and as I resigned my commission, they took it as a joke. And I began then to speak aloud and fearlessly, regardless of their laughter, for it was always kindly and not spiteful laughter. These conversations mostly took place in the evenings, in the company of ladies; women particularly liked listening to me then and they made the men listen.

"But how can I possibly be responsible for all?" every one would laugh in my face. "Can I, for instance, be responsible for you?"

"You may well not know it," I would answer, "since the whole world has long been going on a different line, since we consider the veriest lies as truth and demand the same lies from others. Here I have for once in my life acted sincerely and, well, you all look upon me as a madman. Though you are friendly to me, yet, you see, you all laugh at me."

"But how can we help being friendly to you?" said my hostess, laughing. The room was full of people. All of a sudden the young lady rose, on whose account the duel had been fought and whom only lately I had intended to be my future wife. I had not noticed her coming into the room. She got up, came to me and held out her hand.

"Let me tell you," she said, "that I am the first not to laugh at you, but on the contrary I thank you with tears and express my respect for you for your action then."

Her husband, too, came up and then they all approached me and almost kissed me. My heart was filled with joy, but my attention was especially caught by a middle-aged man who came up to me with the others. I knew him by name already, but had never made his acquaintance nor exchanged a word with him till that evening.

IV: THE MYSTERIOUS VISITOR

He had long been an official in the town; he was in a prominent position, respected by all, rich and had a reputation for benevolence. He subscribed considerable sums to the almshouse and the orphan asylum; he was very charitable, too, in secret, a fact which only became known after his death. He was a man of about fifty, almost stern in appearance and not much given to conversation. He had been married about ten years and his wife, who was still young, had borne him three children. Well, I was sitting alone in my room the following evening, when my door suddenly opened and this gentleman walked in.

I must mention, by the way, that I was no longer living in my former quarters. As soon as I resigned my commission, I took rooms with an old lady, the widow of a government clerk. My landlady's servant waited upon me, for I had moved into her rooms simply because on my return from the duel I had sent Afanasy back to the regiment, as I felt ashamed to look him in the face after my last interview with him. So prone is the man of the world to be ashamed of any righteous action.

"I have," said my visitor, "with great interest listened to you speaking in different houses the last few days and I wanted at last to make your personal acquaintance, so as to talk to you more intimately. Can you, dear sir, grant me this favor?"

"I can, with the greatest pleasure, and I shall look upon it as an honor." I said this, though I felt almost dismayed, so greatly was I impressed from the first moment by the appearance of this man. For though other people had listened to me with interest and attention, no one had come to me before with such a serious, stern and concentrated expression. And now he had come to see me in my own rooms. He sat down.

"You are, I see, a man of great strength of character," he said; "as you have dared to serve the truth, even when by doing so you risked incurring the contempt of all."

"Your praise is, perhaps, excessive," I replied.

"No, it's not excessive," he answered; "believe me, such a course of action is far more difficult than you think. It is that which has impressed me, and it is only on that account that I have come to you," he continued. "Tell me, please, that is if you are not annoyed by my perhaps unseemly curiosity, what were your exact sensations, if you can recall them, at the moment when you made up your mind to ask forgiveness at the duel. Do not think my question frivolous; on the contrary, I have in asking the question a secret motive of my own, which I will perhaps explain to you later on, if it is God's will that we should become more intimately acquainted."

All the while he was speaking, I was looking at him straight into the face and I felt all at once a complete trust in him and great curiosity on my side also, for I felt that there was some strange secret in his soul.

"You ask what were my exact sensations at the moment when I asked my opponent's forgiveness," I answered; "but I had better tell you from the beginning what I have not yet told any one else." And I described all that had passed between Afanasy and me, and how I had bowed down to the ground at his feet. "From that you can see for yourself," I concluded, "that at the time of the duel it was easier for me, for I had made a beginning already at home, and when once I had started on that road, to go farther along it was far from being difficult, but became a source of joy and happiness."

I liked the way he looked at me as he listened. "All that," he said, "is exceedingly interesting. I will come to see you again and again."

And from that time forth he came to see me nearly every evening. And we should have become greater friends, if only he had ever talked of himself. But about himself he scarcely ever said a word, yet continually asked me about myself. In spite of that I became very fond of him and spoke with perfect frankness to him about all my feelings; "for," thought I, "what need have I to know his secrets, since I can see without that that he is a good man? Moreover, though he is such a serious man and my senior, he comes to see a youngster like me and treats me as his equal."

And I learned a great deal that was profitable from him, for he was a man of lofty mind.

"That life is heaven," he said to me suddenly, "that I have long been thinking about"; and all at once he added, "I think of nothing else indeed." He looked at me and smiled. "I am more convinced of it than you are, I will tell you later why."

I listened to him and thought that he evidently wanted to tell me something.

"Heaven," he went on, "lies hidden within all of us—here it lies hidden in me now, and if I will it, it will be revealed to me to-morrow and for all time."

I looked at him; he was speaking with great emotion and gazing mysteriously at me, as if he were questioning me.

"And that we are all responsible to all for all, apart from our own sins, you were quite right in thinking that, and it is wonderful how you could comprehend it in all its significance at once. And in very truth, so soon as men understand that, the Kingdom of Heaven will be for them not a dream, but a living reality."

"And when," I cried out to him bitterly, "when will that come to pass? and will it ever come to pass? Is not it simply a dream of ours?"

"What then, you don't believe it," he said. "You preach it and don't believe it yourself. Believe me, this dream, as you call it, will come to pass without doubt; it will come, but not now, for every process has its law. It's a spiritual, psychological process. To transform the world, to recreate it afresh, men must turn into another path psychologically. Until you have become really, in actual fact, a brother to every one, brotherhood will not come to pass. No sort of scientific teaching, no kind of common interest, will ever teach men to share property and privileges with equal consideration for all. Every one will think his share too small and they will be always envying, complaining and attacking one another. You ask when it will come to pass; it will come to pass, but first we have to go through the period of isolation."

"What do you mean by isolation?" I asked him.

"Why, the isolation that prevails everywhere, above all in our age—it has not fully developed, it has not reached its limit yet. For every one strives to keep his individuality as apart as possible, wishes to secure the greatest possible fullness of life for himself; but meantime all his efforts result not in attaining fullness of life but self-destruction, for instead of self-realization he ends by arriving at complete solitude. All mankind in our age have split up into units, they all keep apart, each in his own groove; each one holds aloof, hides himself and hides what he has, from the rest, and he ends by being repelled by others and repelling them. He heaps up riches by himself and thinks, 'How strong I am now and how secure,' and in his madness he does not understand that the more he heaps up, the more he sinks into self-destructive impotence. For he is accustomed to rely upon himself alone and to cut himself off from the whole; he has trained himself not to believe in the help of others, in men and in humanity, and only trembles for fear he should lose his money and the privileges that he has won for himself. Everywhere in these days men have, in their mockery, ceased to understand that the true security is to be found in social solidarity rather than in isolated individual effort. But this terrible individualism must inevitably have an end, and all will suddenly understand how unnaturally they are separated from one another. It will be the spirit of the time, and people will marvel that they have sat so long in darkness without seeing the light. And then the sign of the Son of Man will be seen in the heavens.... But, until then, we must keep the banner flying. Sometimes even if he has to do it alone, and his conduct seems to be crazy, a man must set an example, and so draw men's souls out of their solitude, and spur them to some act of brotherly love, that the great idea may not die."

Our evenings, one after another, were spent in such stirring and fervent talk. I gave up society and visited my neighbors much less frequently. Besides, my vogue was somewhat over. I say this, not as blame, for they still loved me and treated me good-humoredly, but there's no denying that fashion is a great power in society. I began to regard my mysterious visitor with admiration, for besides enjoying his intelligence, I began to perceive that he was brooding over some plan in his heart, and was preparing himself perhaps for a great deed. Perhaps he liked my not showing curiosity about his secret, not seeking to discover it by direct question nor by insinuation. But I noticed at last, that he seemed to show signs of wanting to tell me something. This had become quite evident, indeed, about a month after he first began to visit me.

"Do you know," he said to me once, "that people are very inquisitive about us in the town and wonder why I come to see you so often. But let them wonder, for *soon all will be explained.*"

Sometimes an extraordinary agitation would come over him, and almost always on such occasions he would get up and go away. Sometimes he would fix a long piercing look upon me, and I thought, "He will say something directly now." But he would suddenly begin talking of something ordinary and familiar. He often complained of headache too.

One day, quite unexpectedly indeed, after he had been talking with great fervor a long time, I saw him suddenly turn pale, and his face worked convulsively, while he stared persistently at me.

"What's the matter?" I said; "do you feel ill?"—he had just been complaining of headache.

"I ... do you know ... I murdered some one."

He said this and smiled with a face as white as chalk. "Why is it he is smiling?" The thought flashed through my mind before I realized anything else. I too turned pale.

"What are you saying?" I cried.

"You see," he said, with a pale smile, "how much it has cost me to say the first word. Now I have said it, I feel I've taken the first step and shall go on."

For a long while I could not believe him, and I did not believe him at that time, but only after he had been to see me three days running and told me all about it. I thought he was mad, but ended by being convinced, to my great grief and amazement. His crime was a great and terrible one.

Fourteen years before, he had murdered the widow of a landowner, a wealthy and handsome young woman who had a house in our town. He fell passionately in love with her, declared his feeling and tried to persuade her to marry him. But she had already given her heart to another man, an officer of noble birth and high rank in the service, who was at that time away at the front, though she was expecting him soon to return. She refused his offer and begged him not to come and see her. After he had ceased to visit her, he took advantage of his knowledge of the house to enter at night through the garden by the roof, at great risk of discovery. But, as often happens, a crime committed with extraordinary audacity is more successful than others.

Entering the garret through the skylight, he went down the ladder, knowing that the door at the bottom of it was sometimes, through the negligence of the servants, left unlocked. He hoped to find it so, and so it was. He made his way in the dark to her bedroom, where a light was burning. As though on purpose, both her maids had gone off to a birthday-party in the same street, without asking leave. The other servants slept in the servants' quarters or in the kitchen on the ground-floor. His passion flamed up at the sight of her asleep, and then vindictive, jealous anger took possession of his heart, and like a drunken man, beside himself, he thrust a knife into her heart, so that she did not even cry out. Then with devilish and criminal cunning he contrived that suspicion should fall on the servants. He was so base as to take her purse, to open her chest with keys from under her pillow, and to take some things from it, doing it all as it might have been done by an ignorant servant, leaving valuable papers and taking only money. He took some of the larger gold things, but left smaller articles that were ten times as valuable. He took with him, too, some things for himself as remembrances, but of that later. Having done this awful deed, he returned by the way he had come.

Neither the next day, when the alarm was raised, nor at any time after in his life, did any one dream of suspecting that he was the criminal. No one indeed knew of his love for her, for he was always reserved and silent and had no friend to whom he would have opened his heart. He was looked upon simply as an acquaintance, and not a very intimate one, of the murdered woman, as for the previous fortnight he had not even visited her.

A serf of hers called Pyotr was at once suspected, and every circumstance confirmed the suspicion. The man knew—indeed his mistress did not conceal the fact—that having to send one of her serfs as a recruit she had decided to send him, as he had no relations and his conduct was unsatisfactory. People had heard him angrily threatening to murder her when he was drunk in a tavern. Two days before her death, he had run away, staying no one knew where in the town. The day after the murder, he was found on the road leading out of the town, dead drunk, with a knife in his pocket, and his right hand happened to be stained with blood. He declared that his nose had been bleeding, but no one believed him. The maids confessed that they had gone to a party and that the street-door had been left open till they returned. And a number of similar details came to light, throwing suspicion on the innocent servant.

They arrested him, and he was tried for the murder; but a week after the arrest, the prisoner fell sick of a fever and died unconscious in the hospital. There the matter ended and the judges and the authorities and every one in the town remained convinced that the crime had been committed by no one but the servant who had died in the hospital. And after that the punishment began.

My mysterious visitor, now my friend, told me that at first he was not in the least troubled by pangs of conscience. He was miserable a long time, but not for that reason; only from regret that he had killed the woman he loved, that she was no more, that in killing her he had killed his love, while the fire of passion was still in his veins. But of the innocent blood he had shed, of the murder of a fellow creature, he scarcely thought. The thought that his victim might have become the wife of another man was insupportable to him, and so, for a long time, he was convinced in his conscience that he could not have acted otherwise.

At first he was worried at the arrest of the servant, but his illness and death soon set his mind at rest, for the man's death was apparently (so he reflected at the time) not owing to his arrest or his fright, but a chill he had taken on the day he ran away, when he had lain all night dead drunk on the damp ground. The theft of the money and other things troubled him little, for he argued that the theft had not been committed for gain but to avert suspicion. The sum stolen was small, and he shortly afterwards subscribed the whole of it, and much more, towards the funds for maintaining an almshouse in the town. He did this on purpose to set his conscience at rest about the theft, and it's a remarkable fact that for a long time he really was at peace—he told me this himself. He entered then upon a career of great activity in the service, volunteered for a difficult and laborious duty, which occupied him two years, and being a man of strong will almost forgot the past. Whenever he recalled it, he tried not to think of it at all. He became active in philanthropy too, founded and helped to maintain many institutions in the town, did a good deal in the two capitals, and in both Moscow and Petersburg was elected a member of philanthropic societies.

At last, however, he began brooding over the past, and the strain of it was too much for him. Then he was attracted by a fine and intelligent girl and soon after married her, hoping that marriage would dispel his lonely depression, and that by entering on a new life and scrupulously doing his duty to his wife and children, he would escape from old memories altogether. But the very opposite of what he expected happened. He began, even in the first month of his marriage, to be continually fretted by the thought, "My wife loves me—but what if she knew?" When she first told him that she would soon bear him a child, he was troubled. "I am giving life, but I have taken life." Children came. "How dare I love them, teach and educate them, how can I talk to them of virtue? I have shed blood." They were splendid children, he longed to caress them; "and I can't look at their innocent candid faces, I am unworthy."

At last he began to be bitterly and ominously haunted by the blood of his murdered victim, by the young life he had destroyed, by the blood that cried out for vengeance. He had begun to have awful dreams. But, being a man of fortitude, he bore his suffering a long time, thinking: "I shall expiate everything by this secret agony." But that hope, too, was vain; the longer it went on, the more intense was his suffering.

He was respected in society for his active benevolence, though every one was overawed by his stern and gloomy character. But the more he was respected, the more intolerable it was for him. He confessed to me that he had thoughts of killing himself. But he began to be haunted by another idea—an idea which he had at first regarded as impossible and unthinkable, though at last it got such a hold on his heart that he could not shake it off. He dreamed of rising up, going out and confessing in the face of all men that he had committed murder. For three years this dream had pursued him, haunting him in different forms. At last he believed with his whole heart that if he confessed his crime, he would heal his soul and would be at peace for ever. But this belief filled his heart with terror, for how could he carry it out? And then came what happened at my duel.

"Looking at you, I have made up my mind."

I looked at him.

"Is it possible," I cried, clasping my hands, "that such a trivial incident could give rise to such a resolution in you?"

"My resolution has been growing for the last three years," he answered, "and your story only gave the last touch to it. Looking at you, I reproached myself and envied you." He said this to me almost sullenly.

"But you won't be believed," I observed; "it's fourteen years ago."

"I have proofs, great proofs. I shall show them."

Then I cried and kissed him.

"Tell me one thing, one thing," he said (as though it all depended upon me), "my wife, my children! My wife may die of grief, and though my children won't lose their rank and property, they'll be a convict's children and for ever! And what a memory, what a memory of me I shall leave in their hearts!"

I said nothing.

"And to part from them, to leave them for ever? It's for ever, you know, for ever!"

I sat still and repeated a silent prayer. I got up at last, I felt afraid.

"Well?" He looked at me.

"Go!" said I, "confess. Everything passes, only the truth remains. Your children will understand, when they grow up, the nobility of your resolution."

He left me that time as though he had made up his mind. Yet for more than a fortnight afterwards, he came to me every evening, still preparing himself, still unable to bring himself to the point. He made my heart ache. One day he would come determined and say fervently:

"I know it will be heaven for me, heaven, the moment I confess. Fourteen years I've been in hell. I want to suffer. I will take my punishment and begin to live. You can pass through the world doing wrong, but there's no turning back. Now I dare not love my neighbor nor even my own children. Good God, my children will understand, perhaps, what my punishment has cost me and will not condemn me! God is not in strength but in truth."

"All will understand your sacrifice," I said to him, "if not at once, they will understand later; for you have served truth, the higher truth, not of the earth."

And he would go away seeming comforted, but next day he would come again, bitter, pale, sarcastic.

"Every time I come to you, you look at me so inquisitively as though to say, 'He has still not confessed!' Wait a bit, don't despise me too much. It's not such an easy thing to do, as you would think. Perhaps I shall not do it at all. You won't go and inform against me then, will you?"

And far from looking at him with indiscreet curiosity, I was afraid to look at him at all. I was quite ill from anxiety, and my heart was full of tears. I could not sleep at night.

"I have just come from my wife," he went on. "Do you understand what the word 'wife' means? When I went out, the children called to me, 'Good-by, father, make haste back to read *The Children's Magazine* with us.' No, you don't understand that! No one is wise from another man's woe."

His eyes were glittering, his lips were twitching. Suddenly he struck the table with his fist so that everything on it danced—it was the first time he had done such a thing, he was such a mild man.

"But need I?" he exclaimed, "must I? No one has been condemned, no one has been sent to Siberia in my place, the man died of fever. And I've been punished by my sufferings for the blood I shed. And I shan't be believed, they won't believe my proofs. Need I confess, need I? I am ready to go on suffering all my life for the blood I have shed, if only my wife and children may be spared. Will it be just to ruin them with me? Aren't we making a mistake? What is right in this case? And will people recognize it, will they appreciate it, will they respect it?"

"Good Lord!" I thought to myself, "he is thinking of other people's respect at such a moment!" And I felt so sorry for him then, that I believe I would have shared his fate if it could have comforted him. I saw he was beside himself. I was aghast, realizing with my heart as well as my mind what such a resolution meant.

"Decide my fate!" he exclaimed again.

"Go and confess," I whispered to him. My voice failed me, but I whispered it firmly. I took up the New Testament from the table, the Russian translation, and showed him the Gospel of St. John, chapter xii. verse 24:

"Verily, verily, I say unto you, except a corn of wheat fall into the ground and die, it abideth alone: but if it die, it bringeth forth much fruit."

I had just been reading that verse when he came in. He read it.

"That's true," he said, but he smiled bitterly. "It's terrible the things you find in those books," he said, after a pause. "It's easy enough to thrust them upon one. And who wrote them? Can they have been written by men?"

"The Holy Spirit wrote them," said I.

"It's easy for you to prate," he smiled again, this time almost with hatred.

I took the book again, opened it in another place and showed him the Epistle to the Hebrews, chapter x. verse 31. He read:

"It is a fearful thing to fall into the hands of the living God."

He read it and simply flung down the book. He was trembling all over.

"An awful text," he said. "There's no denying you've picked out fitting ones." He rose from the chair. "Well!" he said, "good-by, perhaps I shan't come again ... we shall meet in heaven. So I have been for fourteen years 'in the hands of the living God,' that's how one must think of those fourteen years. To-morrow I will beseech those hands to let me go."

I wanted to take him in my arms and kiss him, but I did not dare—his face was contorted and somber. He went away.

"Good God," I thought, "what has he gone to face!" I fell on my knees before the ikon and wept for him before the Holy Mother of God, our swift defender and helper. I was half an hour praying in tears, and it was late, about midnight. Suddenly I saw the door open and he came in again. I was surprised.

"Where have you been?" I asked him.

"I think," he said, "I've forgotten something ... my handkerchief, I think.... Well, even if I've not forgotten anything, let me stay a little."

He sat down. I stood over him.

"You sit down, too," said he.

I sat down. We sat still for two minutes; he looked intently at me and suddenly smiled—I remembered that—then he got up, embraced me warmly and kissed me.

"Remember," he said, "how I came to you a second time. Do you hear, remember it!"

And he went out.

"To-morrow," I thought.

And so it was. I did not know that evening that the next day was his birthday. I had not been out for the last few days, so I had no chance of hearing it from any one. On that day he always had a great gathering, every one in the town went to it. It was the same this time. After dinner he walked into the middle of the room, with a paper in his hand—a formal declaration to the chief of his department who was present. This declaration he read aloud to the whole assembly. It contained a full account of the crime, in every detail.

"I cut myself off from men as a monster. God has visited me," he said in conclusion. "I want to suffer for my sin!"

Then he brought out and laid on the table all the things he had been keeping for fourteen years, that he thought would prove his crime, the jewels belonging to the murdered woman which he had stolen to divert suspicion, a cross and a locket taken from her neck with a portrait of her betrothed in the locket, her notebook and two letters; one from her betrothed, telling her that he would soon be with her, and her unfinished answer left on the table to be sent off next day. He carried off these two letters— what for? Why had he kept them for fourteen years afterwards instead of destroying them as evidence against him?

And this is what happened: every one was amazed and horrified, every one refused to believe it and thought that he was deranged, though all listened with intense curiosity. A few days later it was fully decided and agreed in every house that the unhappy man was mad. The legal authorities could not refuse to take the case up, but they too dropped it. Though the trinkets and letters made them ponder, they decided that even if they did turn out to be authentic, no charge could be based on those alone. Besides, she might have given him those things as a friend, or asked him to take care of them for her. I heard afterwards, however, that the genuineness of the things was proved by the friends and relations of the murdered woman, and that there was no doubt about them. Yet nothing was destined to come of it, after all.

Five days later, all had heard that he was ill and that his life was in danger. The nature of his illness I can't explain, they said it was an affection of the heart. But it became known that the doctors had been induced by his wife to investigate his mental condition also, and had come to the conclusion that it was a case of insanity. I betrayed nothing, though people ran to question me. But when I wanted to visit him, I was for a long while forbidden to do so, above all by his wife.

"It's you who have caused his illness," she said to me; "he was always gloomy, but for the last year people noticed that he was peculiarly excited and did strange things, and now you have been the ruin of him. Your preaching has brought him to this; for the last month he was always with you."

Indeed, not only his wife but the whole town were down upon me and blamed me. "It's all your doing," they said. I was silent and indeed rejoiced at heart, for I saw plainly God's mercy to the man who had turned against himself and punished himself. I could not believe in his insanity.

They let me see him at last, he insisted upon saying good-by to me. I went in to him and saw at once, that not only his days, but his hours were numbered. He was weak, yellow, his hands trembled, he gasped for breath, but his face was full of tender and happy feeling.

"It is done!" he said. "I've long been yearning to see you, why didn't you come?"

I did not tell him that they would not let me see him.

"God has had pity on me and is calling me to Himself. I know I am dying, but I feel joy and peace for the first time after so many years. There was heaven in my heart from the moment I had done what I had to do. Now I dare to love my children and to kiss them. Neither my wife nor the judges, nor any one has believed it. My children will never believe it either. I see in that God's mercy to them. I shall die, and my name will be without a stain for them. And now I feel God near, my heart rejoices as in Heaven ... I have done my duty."

He could not speak, he gasped for breath, he pressed my hand warmly, looking fervently at me. We did not talk for long, his wife kept peeping in at us. But he had time to whisper to me:

"Do you remember how I came back to you that second time, at midnight? I told you to remember it. You know what I came back for? I came to kill you!"

I started.

"I went out from you then into the darkness, I wandered about the streets, struggling with myself. And suddenly I hated you so that I could hardly bear it. Now, I thought, he is all that binds me, and he is my judge. I can't refuse to face my punishment to-morrow, for he knows all. It was not that I was afraid you would betray me (I never even thought of that), but I thought, 'How can I look him in the face if I don't confess?' And if you had been at the other end of the earth, but alive, it would have been all the same, the thought was unendurable that you were alive knowing everything and condemning me. I hated you as though you were the cause, as though you were to blame for everything. I came back to you then, remembering that you had a dagger lying on your table. I sat down and asked you to sit down, and for a whole minute I pondered. If I had killed you, I should have been ruined by that murder even if I had not confessed the other. But I didn't think about that at all, and I didn't want to think of it at that moment. I only hated you and longed to revenge myself on you for everything. The Lord vanquished the devil in my heart. But let me tell you, you were never nearer death."

A week later he died. The whole town followed him to the grave. The chief priest made a speech full of feeling. All lamented the terrible illness that had cut short his days. But all the town was up in arms against me after the funeral, and people even refused to see me. Some, at first a few and afterwards more, began indeed to believe in the truth of his story, and they visited me and questioned me with great interest and eagerness, for man loves to see the downfall and disgrace of the righteous. But I held my tongue, and very shortly after, I left the town, and five months later by God's grace I entered upon the safe and blessed path, praising the unseen finger which had guided me so clearly to it. But I remember in my prayer to this day, the servant of God, Mihail, who suffered so greatly.

V: THE RUSSIAN MONK AND HIS POSSIBLE SIGNIFICANCE

Fathers and teachers, what is the monk? In the cultivated world the word is nowadays pronounced by some people with a jeer, and by others it is used as a term of abuse, and this contempt for the monk is growing. It is true, alas, it is true, that there are many sluggards, gluttons, profligates and insolent beggars among monks. Educated people point to these: "You are idlers, useless members of society, you live on the labor of others, you are shameless beggars." And yet how many meek and humble monks there are, yearning for solitude and fervent prayer in peace! These are less noticed, or passed over in silence. And how surprised men would be if I were to say that from these meek monks, who yearn for solitary prayer, the salvation of Russia will come perhaps once more! For they are in truth made ready in peace and quiet "for the day and the hour, the month and the year." Meanwhile, in their solitude, they keep the image of Christ fair and undefiled, in the purity of God's truth, from the times of the Fathers of old, the Apostles and the martyrs. And when the time comes they will show it to the tottering creeds of the world. That is a great thought. That star will rise out of the East.

That is my view of the monk, and is it false? is it too proud? Look at the worldly and all who set themselves up above the people of God, has not God's image and His truth been distorted in them? They have science; but in science there is nothing but what is the object of sense. The spiritual world, the higher part of man's being is rejected altogether, dismissed with a sort of triumph, even with hatred. The world has proclaimed the reign of freedom, especially of late, but what do we see in this freedom of theirs? Nothing but slavery and self-destruction! For the world says:

"You have desires and so satisfy them, for you have the same rights as the most rich and powerful. Don't be afraid of satisfying them and even multiply your desires." That is the modern doctrine of the world. In that they see freedom. And what follows from this right of multiplication of desires? In the rich, isolation and spiritual suicide; in the poor, envy and murder; for they have been given rights, but have not been shown the means of satisfying their wants. They maintain that the world is getting more and more united, more and more bound together in brotherly community, as it overcomes distance and sets thoughts flying through the air.

Alas, put no faith in such a bond of union. Interpreting freedom as the multiplication and rapid satisfaction of desires, men distort their own nature, for many senseless and foolish desires and habits and ridiculous fancies are fostered in them. They live only for mutual envy, for luxury and ostentation. To have dinners, visits, carriages, rank and slaves to wait on one is looked upon as a necessity, for which life, honor and human feeling are sacrificed, and men even commit suicide if they are unable to satisfy it. We see the same thing among those who are not rich, while the poor drown their unsatisfied need and their envy in drunkenness. But soon they will drink blood instead of wine, they are being led on to it. I ask you is such a man free? I knew one "champion of freedom" who told me himself that, when he was deprived of tobacco in prison, he was so wretched at the privation that he almost went and betrayed his cause for the sake of getting tobacco again! And such a man says, "I am fighting for the cause of humanity."

How can such a one fight? what is he fit for? He is capable perhaps of some action quickly over, but he cannot hold out long. And it's no wonder that instead of gaining freedom they have sunk into slavery, and instead of serving the cause of brotherly love and the union of humanity have fallen, on the contrary, into dissension and isolation, as my mysterious visitor and teacher said to me in my youth. And therefore the idea of the service of humanity, of brotherly love and the solidarity of mankind, is more and more dying out in the world, and indeed this idea is sometimes treated with derision. For how can a man shake off his habits? What can become of him if he is in such bondage to the habit of satisfying the innumerable desires he has created for himself? He is isolated, and what concern has he with the rest of humanity? They have succeeded in accumulating a greater mass of objects, but the joy in the world has grown less.

The monastic way is very different. Obedience, fasting and prayer are laughed at, yet only through them lies the way to real, true freedom. I cut off my superfluous and unnecessary desires, I subdue my proud and wanton will and chastise it with obedience, and with God's help I attain freedom of spirit and with it spiritual joy. Which is most capable of conceiving a great idea and serving it—the rich man in his isolation or the man who has freed himself from the tyranny of material things and habits? The monk is reproached for his solitude, "You have secluded yourself within the walls of the monastery for your own salvation, and have forgotten the brotherly service of humanity!" But we shall see which will be most zealous in the cause of brotherly love. For it is not we, but they, who are in isolation, though they don't see that. Of old, leaders of the people came from among us, and why should they not again? The same meek and humble ascetics will rise up and go out to work for the great cause. The salvation of Russia comes from the people. And the Russian monk has always been on the side of the people. We are isolated only if the people are isolated. The people believe as we do, and an unbelieving reformer will never do anything in Russia, even if he is sincere in heart and a genius. Remember that! The people will meet the atheist and overcome him, and Russia will be one and orthodox. Take care of the peasant and guard his heart. Go on educating him quietly. That's your duty as monks, for the peasant has God in his heart.

VI: OF MASTERS AND SERVANTS, AND OF WHETHER IT IS POSSIBLE FOR THEM TO BE BROTHERS IN THE SPIRIT

Of course, I don't deny that there is sin in the peasants too. And the fire of corruption is spreading visibly, hourly, working from above downwards. The spirit of isolation is coming upon the people too. Money- lenders and devourers of the commune are rising up. Already the merchant grows more and more eager for rank, and strives to show himself cultured though he has not a trace of culture, and to this end meanly despises his old traditions, and is even ashamed of the faith of his fathers. He visits princes, though he is only a peasant corrupted. The peasants are rotting in drunkenness and cannot shake off the habit. And what cruelty to their wives, to their children even! All from drunkenness! I've seen in the factories children of nine years old, frail, rickety, bent and already depraved. The stuffy workshop, the din of machinery, work all day long, the vile language and the drink, the drink—is that what a little child's heart needs? He needs sunshine, childish play, good examples all about him, and at least a little love. There must be no more of this, monks, no more torturing of children, rise up and preach that, make haste, make haste!

But God will save Russia, for though the peasants are corrupted and cannot renounce their filthy sin, yet they know it is cursed by God and that they do wrong in sinning. So that our people still believe in righteousness, have faith in God and weep tears of devotion.

It is different with the upper classes. They, following science, want to base justice on reason alone, but not with Christ, as before, and they have already proclaimed that there is no crime, that there is no sin. And that's consistent, for if you have no God what is the meaning of crime? In Europe the people are already rising up against the rich with violence, and the leaders of the people are everywhere leading them to bloodshed, and teaching them that their wrath is righteous. But their "wrath is accursed, for it is cruel." But God will save Russia as He has saved her many times. Salvation will come from the people, from their faith and their meekness.

Fathers and teachers, watch over the people's faith and this will not be a dream. I've been struck all my life in our great people by their dignity, their true and seemly dignity. I've seen it myself, I can testify to it, I've seen it and marveled at it, I've seen it in spite of the degraded sins and poverty-stricken appearance of our peasantry. They are not servile, and even after two centuries of serfdom they are free in manner and bearing, yet without insolence, and not revengeful and not envious. "You are rich and noble, you are clever and talented, well, be so, God bless you. I respect you, but I know that I too am a man. By the very fact that I respect you without envy I prove my dignity as a man."

In truth if they don't say this (for they don't know how to say this yet), that is how they act. I have seen it myself, I have known it myself, and, would you believe it, the poorer our Russian peasant is, the more noticeable is that serene goodness, for the rich among them are for the most part corrupted already, and much of that is due to our carelessness and indifference. But God will save His people, for Russia is great in her humility. I dream of seeing, and seem to see clearly already, our future. It will come to pass, that even the most corrupt of our rich will end by being ashamed of his riches before the poor, and the poor, seeing his humility, will understand and give way before him, will respond joyfully and kindly to his honorable shame. Believe me that it will end in that; things are moving to that. Equality is to be found only in the spiritual dignity of man, and that will only be understood among us. If we were brothers, there would be fraternity, but before that, they will never agree about the division of wealth. We preserve the image of Christ, and it will shine forth like a precious diamond to the whole world. So may it be, so may it be!

Fathers and teachers, a touching incident befell me once. In my wanderings I met in the town of K. my old orderly, Afanasy. It was eight years since I had parted from him. He chanced to see me in the market-place, recognized me, ran up to me, and how delighted he was! He simply pounced on me: "Master dear, is it you? Is it really you I see?" He took me home with him.

He was no longer in the army, he was married and already had two little children. He and his wife earned their living as costermongers in the market-place. His room was poor, but bright and clean. He made me sit down, set the samovar, sent for his wife, as though my appearance were a festival for them. He brought me his children: "Bless them, Father."

"Is it for me to bless them? I am only a humble monk. I will pray for them. And for you, Afanasy Pavlovitch, I have prayed every day since that day, for it all came from you," said I. And I explained that to him as well as I could. And what do you think? The man kept gazing at me and could not believe that I, his former master, an officer, was now before him in such a guise and position; it made him shed tears.

"Why are you weeping?" said I, "better rejoice over me, dear friend, whom I can never forget, for my path is a glad and joyful one."

He did not say much, but kept sighing and shaking his head over me tenderly.

"What has became of your fortune?" he asked.

"I gave it to the monastery," I answered; "we live in common."

After tea I began saying good-by, and suddenly he brought out half a rouble as an offering to the monastery, and another half-rouble I saw him thrusting hurriedly into my hand: "That's for you in your wanderings, it may be of use to you, Father."

I took his half-rouble, bowed to him and his wife, and went out rejoicing. And on my way I thought: "Here we are both now, he at home and I on the road, sighing and shaking our heads, no doubt, and yet smiling joyfully in the gladness of our hearts, remembering how God brought about our meeting."

I have never seen him again since then. I had been his master and he my servant, but now when we exchanged a loving kiss with softened hearts, there was a great human bond between us. I have thought a great deal about that, and now what I think is this: Is it so inconceivable that that grand and simple-hearted unity might in due time become universal among the Russian people? I believe that it will come to pass and that the time is at hand.

And of servants I will add this: In old days when I was young I was often angry with servants; "the cook had served something too hot, the orderly had not brushed my clothes." But what taught me better then was a thought of my dear brother's, which I had heard from him in childhood: "Am I worth it, that another should serve me and be ordered about by me in his poverty and ignorance?" And I wondered at the time that such simple and self- evident ideas should be so slow to occur to our minds.

It is impossible that there should be no servants in the world, but act so that your servant may be freer in spirit than if he were not a servant. And why cannot I be a servant to my servant and even let him see it, and that without any pride on my part or any mistrust on his? Why should not my servant be like my own kindred, so that I may take him into my family and rejoice in doing so? Even now this can be done, but it will lead to the grand unity of men in the future, when a man will not seek servants for himself, or desire to turn his fellow creatures into servants as he does now, but on the contrary, will long with his whole heart to be the servant of all, as the Gospel teaches.

And can it be a dream, that in the end man will find his joy only in deeds of light and mercy, and not in cruel pleasures as now, in gluttony, fornication, ostentation, boasting and envious rivalry of one with the other? I firmly believe that it is not and that the time is at hand. People laugh and ask: "When will that time come and does it look like coming?" I believe that with Christ's help we shall accomplish this great thing. And how many ideas there have been on earth in the history of man which were unthinkable ten years before they appeared! Yet when their destined hour had come, they came forth and spread over the whole earth. So it will be with us, and our people will shine forth in the world, and all men will say: "The stone which the builders rejected has become the corner-stone of the building."

And we may ask the scornful themselves: If our hope is a dream, when will you build up your edifice and order things justly by your intellect alone, without Christ? If they declare that it is they who are advancing towards unity, only the most simple-hearted among them believe it, so that one may positively marvel at such simplicity. Of a truth, they have more fantastic dreams than we. They aim at justice, but, denying Christ, they will end by flooding the earth with blood, for blood cries out for blood, and he that taketh up the sword shall perish by the sword. And if it were not for Christ's covenant, they would slaughter one another down to the last two men on earth. And those two last men would not be able to restrain each other in their pride, and the one would slay the other and then himself. And that would come to pass, were it not for the promise of Christ that for the sake of the humble and meek the days shall be shortened.

While I was still wearing an officer's uniform after my duel, I talked about servants in general society, and I remember every one was amazed at me. "What!" they asked, "are we to make our servants sit down on the sofa and offer them tea?" And I answered them: "Why not, sometimes at least?" Every one laughed. Their question was frivolous and my answer was not clear; but the thought in it was to some extent right.

VII: OF PRAYER, OF LOVE, AND OF CONTACT WITH OTHER WORLDS

Young man, be not forgetful of prayer. Every time you pray, if your prayer is sincere, there will be new feeling and new meaning in it, which will give you fresh courage, and you will understand that prayer is an education. Remember, too, every day, and whenever you can, repeat to yourself, "Lord, have mercy on all who appear before Thee to-day." For every hour and every moment thousands of men leave life on this earth, and their souls appear before God. And how many of them depart in solitude, unknown, sad, dejected that no one mourns for them or even knows whether they have lived or not! And behold, from the other end of the earth perhaps, your prayer for their rest will rise up to God though you knew them not nor they you. How touching it must be to a soul standing in dread before the Lord to feel at that instant that, for him too, there is one to pray, that there is a fellow creature left on earth to love him too! And God will look on you both more graciously, for if you have had so much pity on him, how much will He have pity Who is infinitely more loving and merciful than you! And He will forgive him for your sake.

Brothers, have no fear of men's sin. Love a man even in his sin, for that is the semblance of Divine Love and is the highest love on earth. Love all God's creation, the whole and every grain of sand in it. Love every leaf, every ray of God's light. Love the animals, love the plants, love everything. If you love everything, you will perceive the divine mystery in things. Once you perceive it, you will begin to comprehend it better every day. And you will come at last to love the whole world with an all-embracing love. Love the animals: God has given them the rudiments of thought and joy untroubled. Do not trouble it, don't harass them, don't deprive them of their happiness, don't work against God's intent. Man, do not pride yourself on superiority to the animals; they are without sin, and you, with your greatness, defile the earth by your appearance on it, and leave the traces of your foulness after you—alas, it is true of almost every one of us! Love children especially, for they too are sinless like the angels; they live to soften and purify our hearts and as it were to guide us. Woe to him who offends a child! Father Anfim taught me to love children. The kind, silent man used often on our wanderings to spend the farthings given us on sweets and cakes for the children. He could not pass by a child without emotion. That's the nature of the man.

At some thoughts one stands perplexed, especially at the sight of men's sin, and wonders whether one should use force or humble love. Always decide to use humble love. If you resolve on that once for all, you may subdue the whole world. Loving humility is marvelously strong, the strongest of all things, and there is nothing else like it.

Every day and every hour, every minute, walk round yourself and watch yourself, and see that your image is a seemly one. You pass by a little child, you pass by, spiteful, with ugly words, with wrathful heart; you may not have noticed the child, but he has seen you, and your image, unseemly and ignoble, may remain in his defenseless heart. You don't know it, but you may have sown an evil seed in him and it may grow, and all because you were not careful before the child, because you did not foster in yourself a careful, actively benevolent love. Brothers, love is a teacher; but one must know how to acquire it, for it is hard to acquire, it is dearly bought, it is won slowly by long labor. For we must love not only occasionally, for a moment, but for ever. Every one can love occasionally, even the wicked can.

My brother asked the birds to forgive him; that sounds senseless, but it is right; for all is like an ocean, all is flowing and blending; a touch in one place sets up movement at the other end of the earth. It may be senseless to beg forgiveness of the birds, but birds would be happier at your side—a little happier, anyway—and children and all animals, if you were nobler than you are now. It's all like an ocean, I tell you. Then you would pray to the birds too, consumed by an all-embracing love, in a sort of transport, and pray that they too will forgive you your sin. Treasure this ecstasy, however senseless it may seem to men.

My friends, pray to God for gladness. Be glad as children, as the birds of heaven. And let not the sin of men confound you in your doings. Fear not that it will wear away your work and hinder its being accomplished. Do not say, "Sin is mighty, wickedness is mighty, evil environment is mighty, and we are lonely and helpless, and evil environment is wearing us away and hindering our good work from being done." Fly from that dejection, children! There is only one means of salvation, then take yourself and make yourself responsible for all men's sins, that is the truth, you know, friends, for as soon as you sincerely make yourself responsible for everything and for all men, you will see at once that it is really so, and that you are to blame for every one and for all things. But throwing your own indolence and impotence on others you will end by sharing the pride of Satan and murmuring against God.

Of the pride of Satan what I think is this: it is hard for us on earth to comprehend it, and therefore it is so easy to fall into error and to share it, even imagining that we are doing something grand and fine. Indeed, many of the strongest feelings and movements of our nature we cannot comprehend on earth. Let not that be a stumbling-block, and think not that it may serve as a justification to you for anything. For the Eternal Judge asks of you what you can comprehend and not what you cannot. You will know that yourself hereafter, for you will behold all things truly then and will not dispute them. On earth, indeed, we are as it were astray, and if it were not for the precious image of Christ before us, we should be undone and altogether lost, as was the human race before the flood. Much on earth is hidden from us, but to make up for that we have been given a precious mystic sense of our living bond with the other world, with the higher heavenly world, and the roots of our thoughts and feelings are not here but in other worlds. That is why the philosophers say that we cannot apprehend the reality of things on earth.

God took seeds from different worlds and sowed them on this earth, and His garden grew up and everything came up that could come up, but what grows lives and is alive only through the feeling of its contact with other mysterious worlds. If that feeling grows weak or is destroyed in you, the heavenly growth will die away in you. Then you will be indifferent to life and even grow to hate it. That's what I think.

VIII: CAN A MAN JUDGE HIS FELLOW CREATURES? FAITH TO THE END

Remember particularly that you cannot be a judge of any one. For no one can judge a criminal, until he recognizes that he is just such a criminal as the man standing before him, and that he perhaps is more than all men to blame for that crime. When he understands that, he will be able to be a judge. Though that sounds absurd, it is true. If I had been righteous myself, perhaps there would have been no criminal standing before me. If you can take upon yourself the crime of the criminal your heart is judging, take it at once, suffer for him yourself, and let him go without reproach. And even if the law itself makes you his judge, act in the same spirit so far as possible, for he will go away and condemn himself more bitterly than you have done. If, after your kiss, he goes away untouched, mocking at you, do not let that be a stumbling-block to you. It shows his time has not yet come, but it will come in due course. And if it come not, no matter; if not he, then another in his place will understand and suffer, and judge and condemn himself, and the truth will be fulfilled. Believe that, believe it without doubt; for in that lies all the hope and faith of the saints.

Work without ceasing. If you remember in the night as you go to sleep, "I have not done what I ought to have done," rise up at once and do it. If the people around you are spiteful and callous and will not hear you, fall down before them and beg their forgiveness; for in truth you are to blame for their not wanting to hear you. And if you cannot speak to them in their bitterness, serve them in silence and in humility, never losing hope. If all men abandon you and even drive you away by force, then when you are left alone fall on the earth and kiss it, water it with your tears and it will bring forth fruit even though no one has seen or heard you in your solitude. Believe to the end, even if all men went astray and you were left the only one faithful; bring your offering even then and praise God in your loneliness. And if two of you are gathered together—then there is a whole world, a world of living love. Embrace each other tenderly and praise God, for if only in you two His truth has been fulfilled.

If you sin yourself and grieve even unto death for your sins or for your sudden sin, then rejoice for others, rejoice for the righteous man, rejoice that if you have sinned, he is righteous and has not sinned.

If the evil-doing of men moves you to indignation and overwhelming distress, even to a desire for vengeance on the evil-doers, shun above all things that feeling. Go at once and seek suffering for yourself, as though you were yourself guilty of that wrong. Accept that suffering and bear it and your heart will find comfort, and you will understand that you too are guilty, for you might have been a light to the evil-doers, even as the one man sinless, and you were not a light to them. If you had been a light, you would have lightened the path for others too, and the evil-doer might perhaps have been saved by your light from his sin. And even though your light was shining, yet you see men were not saved by it, hold firm and doubt not the power of the heavenly light. Believe that if they were not saved, they will be saved hereafter. And if they are not saved hereafter, then their sons will be saved, for your light will not die even when you are dead. The righteous man departs, but his light remains. Men are always saved after the death of the deliverer. Men reject their prophets and slay them, but they love their martyrs and honor those whom they have slain. You are working for the whole, you are acting for the future. Seek no reward, for great is your reward on this earth: the spiritual joy which is only vouchsafed to the righteous man. Fear not the great nor the mighty, but be wise and ever serene. Know the measure, know the times, study that. When you are left alone, pray. Love to throw yourself on the earth and kiss it. Kiss the earth and love it with an unceasing, consuming love. Love all men, love everything. Seek that rapture and ecstasy. Water the earth with the tears of your joy and love those tears. Don't be ashamed of that ecstasy, prize it, for it is a gift of God and a great one; it is not given to many but only to the elect.

IX: OF HELL AND HELL FIRE, A MYSTIC REFLECTION

Fathers and teachers, I ponder, "What is hell?" I maintain that it is the suffering of being unable to love. Once in infinite existence, immeasurable in time and space, a spiritual creature was given on his coming to earth, the power of saying, "I am and I love." Once, only once, there was given him a moment of active *living* love, and for that was earthly life given him, and with it times and seasons. And that happy creature rejected the priceless gift, prized it and loved it not, scorned it and remained callous. Such a one, having left the earth, sees Abraham's bosom and talks with Abraham as we are told in the parable of the rich man and Lazarus, and beholds heaven and can go up to the Lord. But that is just his torment, to rise up to the Lord without ever having loved, to be brought close to those who have loved when he has despised their love. For he sees clearly and says to himself, "Now I have understanding, and though I now thirst to love, there will be nothing great, no sacrifice in my love, for my earthly life is over, and Abraham will not come even with a drop of living water (that is the gift of earthly active life) to cool the fiery thirst of spiritual love which burns in me now, though I despised it on earth; there is no more life for me and will be no more time! Even though I would gladly give my life for others, it can never be, for that life is passed which can be sacrificed for love, and now there is a gulf fixed between that life and this existence."

They talk of hell fire in the material sense. I don't go into that mystery and I shun it. But I think if there were fire in material sense, they would be glad of it, for I imagine that in material agony, their still greater spiritual agony would be forgotten for a moment. Moreover, that spiritual agony cannot be taken from them, for that suffering is not external but within them. And if it could be taken from them, I think it would be bitterer still for the unhappy creatures. For even if the righteous in Paradise forgave them, beholding their torments, and called them up to heaven in their infinite love, they would only multiply their torments, for they would arouse in them still more keenly a flaming thirst for responsive, active and grateful love which is now impossible. In the timidity of my heart I imagine, however, that the very recognition of this impossibility would serve at last to console them. For accepting the love of the righteous together with the impossibility of repaying it, by this submissiveness and the effect of this humility, they will attain at last, as it were, to a certain semblance of that active love which they scorned in life, to something like its outward expression.... I am sorry, friends and brothers, that I cannot express this clearly. But woe to those who have slain themselves on earth, woe to the suicides! I believe that there can be none more miserable than they. They tell us that it is a sin to pray for them and outwardly the Church, as it were, renounces them, but in my secret heart I believe that we may pray even for them. Love can never be an offense to Christ. For such as those I have prayed inwardly all my life, I confess it, fathers and teachers, and even now I pray for them every day.

Oh, there are some who remain proud and fierce even in hell, in spite of their certain knowledge and contemplation of the absolute truth; there are some fearful ones who have given themselves over to Satan and his proud spirit entirely. For such, hell is voluntary and ever consuming; they are tortured by their own choice. For they have cursed themselves, cursing God and life. They live upon their vindictive pride like a starving man in the desert sucking blood out of his own body. But they are never satisfied, and they refuse forgiveness, they curse God Who calls them. They cannot behold the living God without hatred, and they cry out that the God of life should be annihilated, that God should destroy Himself and His own creation. And they will burn in the fire of their own wrath for ever and yearn for death and annihilation. But they will not attain to death....

EPILOGUE

Here Alexey Fyodorovitch Karamazov's manuscript ends. I repeat, it is incomplete and fragmentary. Biographical details, for instance, cover only Father Zossima's earliest youth. Of his teaching and opinions we find brought together sayings evidently uttered on very different occasions. His utterances during the last few hours have not been kept separate from the rest, but their general character can be gathered from what we have in Alexey Fyodorovitch's manuscript.

ABOUT THE AUTHOR

Dostoevsky's life was marked by both personal and professional challenges. At an early age, he was exposed to literature and grew enamored with the written word. After completing his education in engineering, he decided to pursue a career in writing, which led to his first novel, "Poor Folk," gaining critical acclaim. However, his rising literary career took a tragic turn when he was sentenced to death in 1849 for participating in a radical political group.

Through a twist of fate, Dostoevsky's sentence was commuted to four years of hard labor in Siberia, an experience that profoundly influenced his subsequent works. It was during this period of exile that he began to explore themes of redemption, guilt, and spirituality, which would become central to his literary masterpieces.

Upon his return to St. Petersburg, Dostoevsky faced financial difficulties and struggled with gambling addiction, a personal battle that left a lasting impact on his life and writings. Despite these hardships, he continued to write and publish his works, with "Crime and Punishment" and "The Idiot" solidifying his reputation as a literary genius.

However, it was Dostoevsky's final novel, "The Brothers Karamazov," published in 1880, that stands as his magnum opus and a testament to his profound insight into the human soul. This monumental work delves into complex family dynamics, spiritual dilemmas, and the existential search for meaning. With its richly drawn characters, philosophical inquiries, and exploration of moral responsibility, "The Brothers Karamazov" remains a timeless masterpiece that continues to captivate readers across generations.

Made in United States
North Haven, CT
03 July 2023